PATRICK'S PERFECT PET

Annalena McAfee's first job was as assistant editor on the comic books *Spiderman* and *The Incredible Hulk*. She is now a journalist and writer, who has written several books for children, including the acclaimed Walker picture book, *The Visitors Who Came To Stay*, illustrated by Hans Christian Andersen Award-winner, Anthony Browne. Annalena is married to the novelist Ian McEwan, and lives in north London.

ANNALENA MCAFEE

Patrick's Perfect Pet

Illustrations by Arthur Robins

WALKER BOOKS
AND SUBSIDIARIES
LONDON • BOSTON • SYDNEY

For Arun, Jai and Oscar

First published 2002 by
Walker Books Ltd, 87 Vauxhall Walk
London SE11 5HJ

2 4 6 8 10 9 7 5 3 1

Text © 2002 Annalena McAfee
Illustrations © 2002 Arthur Robins

This book has been typeset in Garamond

Printed and bound in Great Britain by The Guernsey Press Co. Ltd

British Library Cataloguing in Publication Data:
a catalogue record for this book
is available from the British Library

ISBN 0-7445-8911-8

CONTENTS

CHAPTER ONE

Patrick Foggett had always wanted a pet.

"No, dogs are too messy," said his mum. "And they need too much exercise."

"No, cats scratch the furniture," said his dad. "And they shed hairs."

"No, spiders are too scary," said his big sister, Sal.

"What about a parrot?"
"Too noisy."

"A frog?"
"Too slimy."

"A donkey?"
"Too big."

"A pig?"
"Too smelly."

"A mouse?"
"Not in this house."

10

"A moose?"

"Don't be silly."

"A ring-tailed raccoon?"

"Be quiet and eat your breakfast!"

As Patrick lifted his spoon to tap his egg, the strangest thing happened... He noticed the shell was already cracked, and the crack was getting bigger.

First, one tiny green foot
appeared, then another.

A little green head emerged with
blinking eyes and a shy smile.

The creature stepped out of the shell and stared timidly up at Patrick.

3

"Look Mum! Look Dad! Look Sal!
A baby dinosaur. Can we keep it?"

"Well, I suppose it's not too big,"
said Dad.

"It wouldn't need much
exercise," said Mum. "And it seems
quite clean."

"It's not really scary," said Sal.

"Please can we keep it?" begged Patrick.

"Oh, all right," said Mrs Foggett, who secretly thought it was rather a sweet little thing.

"But as soon as that pet of yours puts one foot wrong, out it goes," said Mr Foggett, who was thinking that for a previously extinct prehistoric animal, it was really quite cute.

"And I don't want it coming
anywhere near my room and
messing my things up," said Sal,
who privately wished the tiny
dinosaur was hers.

"Don't worry," said Patrick.
"My little dinosaur will be the best-
behaved pet in the world."

Cupping the creature gently in his hands, he ran upstairs to his bedroom to prepare a nest for his perfect pet.

CHAPTER TWO

Soon, it was as if Tiny the dinosaur had always lived with Patrick.

They got into a pleasant routine. After breakfast – a single raisin, or maybe a currant, for Tiny – Patrick would slip his pet into his pocket and take him to school.

Everyone wondered why Patrick seemed to whisper into his hand a lot.

His mum and dad didn't mind Tiny going to school. Their son's schoolwork had improved since he got a pet – and his bedroom had never been so tidy.

"Tiny needs a regular timetable," said Patrick. "And most animals flourish in a pleasant, ordered environment."

All in all, the Foggetts concluded, Patrick's pet seemed to be a good influence. And he was a pleasure to have around.

CHAPTER THREE

Gradually, Tiny began to grow, and
Patrick had to carry him to school
in his rucksack. His perfect pet
could no longer be kept a secret,
but he was such a good-natured
animal that all the children – even
the school bully – loved to play
with Tiny.

And the teachers thought such a well-behaved creature set a fine example to the children.

But Patrick always made sure that Tiny didn't get exhausted by all the attention. "Don't crowd him," he told his schoolfriends. "He needs his space, just like you and me."

At home, Tiny began to help with the chores: washing dishes, a little dusting, carrying out the rubbish, that sort of thing.

He was always polite to the
neighbours, and spent at least half
an hour every day picking up litter
in the Foggetts' street.

"Tiny's certainly eating more," said Mrs Foggett. "But he's no trouble at all."

"He's needing more exercise these days," said Mr Foggett. "But it does us the world of good, too."

Tiny was also proving to be a skilled gardener. He planted some shrubs with huge, bell-shaped flowers that no one knew the name of. They grew nearly as fast as he did.

He turned the garden pond –
until then more of a puddle – into
a waterfall, and put up a hammock
for Sal between two sweet-smelling
vines.

Patrick always applauded his
pet's efforts. "Good dinosaur,"
he would say, patting Tiny's head.

"Tiny has his uses," said Sal.

What she meant was that she, like everyone else in Patrick's family, couldn't imagine life without him now – even as the perfect pet continued to grow.

CHAPTER FOUR

By now, Tiny was much too big to fit into Patrick's rucksack, and would walk alongside him to school.

Patrick patiently taught the young dinosaur road safety. They got some funny looks from passing strangers, and cars tended to screech to a halt when they stepped off the pavement.

But once people got over their initial surprise, they were always pleased to see Tiny.

At school, he
began to help the
PE teacher organize
games and, with the
caretaker, started to brighten up the
school's shabby playground.

Patrick's pet was particularly welcomed by the geography and biology teachers, who said he always made a valuable contribution to their lessons.

"You're the cleverest pet in the whole world," said Patrick, marvelling at Tiny's knowledge of evolutionary theory.

At home, Tiny helped with the cooking and shopping. He was very useful in the supermarket, where he reached down tins from the top shelf and steered the loaded trolleys through the aisles. The check-out ladies always had a friendly word for him.

"Tiny is beginning to eat us out of house and home," said Mr and Mrs Foggett proudly.

CHAPTER FIVE

Tiny built an adventure playground for Patrick, with tree swings and a rope bridge over the waterfall. Then, with the artful use of seashells, stuffed parrots and indoor palm trees, he transformed Sal's bedroom into a jungle queen's grotto.

Sometimes, Patrick worried that his pet seemed a little sad. Tiny would go off his food and Patrick would find him in the garden at midnight, gazing at the moon.

Patrick, knowing
that it's sometimes
better to show
your love in
wordless ways,
would gently
stroke his pet
until Tiny
heaved a last
sigh and came
indoors for
the night.
Generally, though,
he was a cheerful and
affectionate dinosaur and
continued to make himself useful
around the house and at school.

Eventually, Tiny grew so big that Patrick had to move out of his room to make space for him. "My pet comes first," insisted Patrick. "I can sleep anywhere."

Everyone was surprised that Sal didn't mind sharing her room with Patrick. "Tiny has to have somewhere to curl up," she said.

As his perfect pet grew larger,
Patrick became even more fond of
him. "There's more of you to love
and take care of," Patrick reassured
his dinosaur. "The bigger the
better. The more the merrier."

Tiny didn't mind Patrick's friends taking turns to ride him. As he grew, his appetite was increasing every day. He now did all the shopping, and had become an expert cook – barbecues were his speciality.

The exotic fruit trees he had planted began to yield rich crops, which the whole family enjoyed.

"Makes a nice change from tinned pears," said Mrs Foggett.

CHAPTER SIX

When it became clear that Patrick's room was going to be too small for Tiny, Mr and Mrs Foggett offered their bigger bedroom.

"We can sleep on the sofa," said Mrs Foggett.

"A change is as good as a rest," said Mr Foggett.

But Tiny politely declined and
moved into the garden, making a
nest for himself among the dense
foliage. The garden shed had to go
to make room for the expanding
dinosaur.

"I never liked that shed anyway,"
said Mr Foggett, who was delighted
with the deluxe tree house Tiny
built him instead.

Everyone realized Tiny was too
big to sit in the classroom any
longer when he got up to answer a
biology question and his head
went through the ceiling.

"Easily done," said the caretaker. Tiny helped him repair the hole, but after that he spent his days in the playground, keeping the sports equipment in order, replanting the school flower beds, repairing the roof and building a swimming pool that became the envy of children for hundreds of miles around.

CHAPTER SEVEN

But, like many good things and
most bad things too, it had to end.
What was it – what single incident
finally prompted Tiny's departure?
Patrick Foggett still asks himself
that question, standing in the
garden at midnight and gazing at
the moon, just as Tiny had done on
those melancholy nights long ago.

What was "the straw that broke the dinosaur's back", as Mrs Foggett said?

It wasn't the time when Tiny stepped back from the swimming pool to admire the new water chute and accidentally sat on the headmistress's car.

"Accidents will happen," said the headmistress. "And it's a lovely water chute. I've tried it myself."

It wasn't the day that Tiny, dozing in the garden, dreamed he was caught in a tropical storm and broke the neighbour's fence with his thrashing tail.

The neighbour was very nice, considering. "It never rains but it pours," he said mysteriously.

It wasn't the afternoon that Tiny
caused chaos in the supermarket
when he got wedged between
Frozen Foods and Tinned Veg.

"No problem," said the
manageress. "We'll get a forklift
truck and shift these aisles. We'll
have him out in no time."

Nor was it the day when the police had to be called to sort out the traffic because Tiny got stuck under a motorway bridge.

"No harm done, eh," said the police inspector as the helicopter lifted off a section of the bridge.

It wasn't even the moment that everyone realized Tiny was too big to live in the garden any more.

"Don't worry, we'll soon fix that," said Mr Foggett. "We'll just knock down the back extension and expand the garden. We only need one bathroom, and we have so many barbecues these days we don't really need a kitchen."

No, it was Tiny himself who made the decision. He had to go.

"It was time," Patrick's mum said later, by way of explanation, "to be with his own kind." Tiny was going back to that hidden corner of the world where dinosaurs still roam free.

CHAPTER EIGHT

The whole town turned out to bid him a tearful farewell. But no one was more unhappy than Patrick.

"You've been a truly perfect pet," Patrick sniffed. "I'm going to miss you so much."

Tiny's own huge eyes were filled with tears as he waved Patrick a final farewell. Mrs Foggett worried that if he blinked, "we'll all be soaked to the skin".

With one last forlorn backward glance, Tiny walked towards the distant hills,

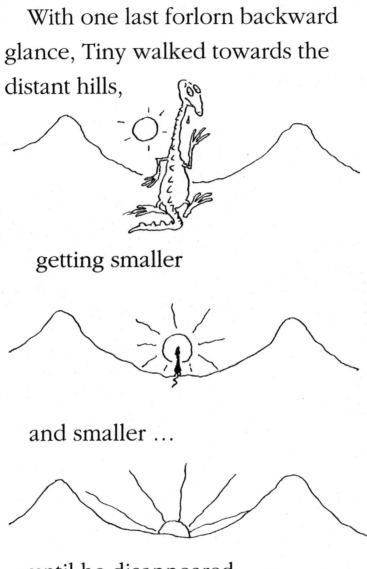

getting smaller

and smaller …

until he disappeared.

Patrick ran to his room sobbing.
There, on his bed, was a box
tied with a bow.

It was a present from Tiny.
To Patrick, the Perfect Pet Owner,
said the label.

Inside the box was an egg.
Its shell was cracked, and the crack
was getting bigger, and bigger...

More *Sprinters* for you to enjoy!

- *Little Stupendo Flies High* Jon Blake   0-7445-5970-7
- *Captain Abdul's Pirate School* Colin McNaughton 0-7445-5242-7
- *The Ghost in Annie's Room* Philippa Pearce   0-7445-5993-6
- *Molly and the Beanstalk* Pippa Goodhart   0-7445-5981-2
- *Taking the Cat's Way Home* Jan Mark   0-7445-8268-7
- *The Finger-eater* Dick King-Smith   0-7445-8269-5
- *Care of Henry* Anne Fine   0-7445-8270-9
- *The Haunting of Pip Parker* Anne Fine   0-7445-8294-6
- *Cup Final Kid* Martin Waddell   0-7445-8297-0
- *Lady Long-legs* Jan Mark   0-7445-8296-2
- *Ronnie and the Giant Millipede* Jenny Nimmo   0-7445-8298-9
- *Emmelina and the Monster* June Crebbin   0-7445-8904-5
- *Posh Watson* Gillian Cross   0-7445-8271-7
- *Impossible Parents* Arthur Robins   0-7445-9022-1
- *Holly and the Skyboard* Ian Whybrow   0-7445-9021-3
- *Patrick's Perfect Pet* Annalena McAfee   0-7445-8911-8
- *Me and My Big Mouse* Simon Cheshire   0-7445-5982-0
- *No Tights for George!* June Crebbin   0-7445-5999-5

All at £3.99